RHINOCEROS   BONGO   KIDOGO'S MAMA

LION   HIPPOPOTAMUS   SHOEBILL   LEOPARD

KIDOGO

For Noel, my own Kidogo

Note: The word *kidogo* means *little* in Kiswahili. It is pronounced kee-DOE-go.
Kidogo kidogo means *little by little*.

First published in Great Britain in 2005 by Bloomsbury Publishing Plc
38 Soho Square, London, W1D 3HB
First published in America by Bloomsbury Children's Books USA, New York
Text and illustrations copyright © Anik McGrory 2005
Typeset in TL Pierre Bonnard and Cooper Old Style Light.
The art was created with pencil and watercolor.
Designed by Marikka Tamura.
The moral right of the author/illustrator has been asserted
A CIP catalogue record of this book is available from the British Library
ISBN 0 7475 7634 3
Printed by Tien Wah Press in Singapore
1 3 5 7 9 10 8 6 4 2
All papers used by Bloomsbury Publishing are natural, recyclable products
made from wood grown in well-managed forests. The manufacturing processes
conform to the environmental regulations of the country of origin.

KIDOGO

ANIK McGRORY

BLOOMSBURY
CHILDREN'S
BOOKS

Kidogo lived in a world that was vast.
He walked under a mountain bigger than the clouds.

He played on endless fields of rippling gold.

And he slept through nights that
were deeper than his dreams.

He was very small...for an elephant.

His aunties helped
him reach tender
acacia leaves.

His cousins helped him cross
the flooding river.

His mama helped him with his dust bath,
although he wasn't sure he needed one.

But Kidogo didn't want help.
He didn't want to be the smallest.
So he went off to find someone in the world
who was just as small as he.

He looked in the woodlands.

He looked in the flooding river.

He looked on the plains.

He looked until he knew it was true...

...he was the smallest animal in all the world.

He stopped, lost and alone,
with no place left to look.

He sat and decided.

He wouldn't need anyone else—
big or small.

He would find his own
acacia leaves.

He would cross the river by himself.

He would make his own dust bath.
But as the dust fell around him,
there was a tickling and an itching on
his ears and tail and legs and nose.

He swiped and rolled

and brushed

and blew...

...until, finally, the itching stopped.
And there, as he looked down,
was an animal smaller than
he had ever imagined.
Soon he was
surrounded by
tiny animals.

He helped them reach tender acacia leaves.

He helped them cross a flooding river.

He helped them with a dust bath,
although they weren't sure they needed one.

He followed the insects on a march down
the riverbank, through the woodlands,
across the plains, and back to his very own home.

Kidogo saw the insects and the mountains,
little and big. There were his cousins,
his aunties, and his mama.

And Kidogo knew he wasn't too small after all.

He was just right...for a little elephant.